Pipsy and Friends

By Marian Ivens

Illustrated by Andrew N. Dale

AuthorHouse™ UK
1663 Liberty Drive
Bloomington, IN 47403 USA
www.authorhouse.co.uk
Phone: 0800 047 8203 (Domestic TFN)
+44 1908 723714 (International)

Because of the dynamic nature of the Internet, any web addresses or links contained in this book may have changed since publication and may no longer be valid. The views expressed in this work are solely those of the author and do not necessarily reflect the views of the publisher, and the publisher hereby disclaims any responsibility for them.

Any people depicted in stock imagery provided by Getty Images are models, and such images are being used for illustrative purposes only.
Certain stock imagery © Getty Images.

This book is printed on acid-free paper.

ISBN: 978-1-7283-5359-3 (sc)
978-1-7283-5358-6 (e)

Print information available on the last page.

Published by AuthorHouse 05/22/2020

authorHOUSE®

Thank you to ...

Emma for reading "Pipsy" to Matthew and Edward.

Nick for unstinting encouragement.

David S. for computer expertise.

Andrew for inspired illustrations.

James, Louise and Dominic, always ready to cheer me on.

To Mark C. for his timely guidance.

To Mark E. for getting "Pipsy and Friends" into print.

Marian

It was very late summer and just one small apple was left behind on the old apple tree.

"I wonder where my brothers and sisters have gone?" he sighed.

Suddenly, to his surprise, Pipsy, for that was his name, felt the old tree shake and sway.

Swing and sway! Swing and sway! Swing, and…

BOOMPH!

Pipsy bounced to the ground…

OUCH!

He looked up to see a big, soft, grey nose.

"Who are you?" said The Grey Nose. "You look very good to eat!"

"Oh, please don't eat me! I am so small. Not much for you!"

"Mmmmmmmm," said The Grey Nose. "I will put you in the sun on the orchard wall. You will get big and sweet there!"

So Ned, the grey-nosed donkey, gently put Pipsy on the wall.

But when the sun set Pipsy shivered.

BRRRR........

A tear rolled down his rosy cheek. Splash!

"Oh!" cried a little voice. Pipsy jumped and tumbled off the wall.

"Oh!" cried the little voice again, "That was a heavy drop of rain!"

Pipsy saw a funny little face smiling at him.

"Hello, I'm Oscar Snail. I hope you didn't hurt yourself falling on my roof!"

"I am really sorry Oscar, but I feel so alone and it is getting dark!"

"Don't cry," said Oscar. "Climb on my back. I have an idea."

Very slowly Oscar, with Pipsy on his back, slid across the garden.

"Now you roll under there and go to sleep," said Oscar. "Sleep tight!"

When the sun came up Pipsy wondered where Oscar had put him to bed.

He could see a wooden wheel and two wooden handles and a brightly painted wooden roof.

But, before Pipsy could decide what kind of house it was, a big bright light flashed across the sky and there was a loud noise, then *pit pat, pit pat, pitter patter, pitter patter*, faster and faster.

Then, something as fast as a rocket flew across the orchard … and into Pipsy's house!

"Miaowwww… Ugh!" mewled Silas, the tiger cat.
"I hate getting wet!"

"Good morning," said Pipsy. "Nice to meet you."

"Let's go where it's warm," said Silas. "Come on!"

Silas carefully picked him up, and carried him across the orchard to the back door of the farmhouse.

Silas nosed the door open and then softly climbed the back stairs to the attic.

"There you go!" Silas purred, as he set Pipsy down on the very top stair.

"Oh, thank you so much, I am ....!"

... but Pipsy could say no more because his mouth had dropped open in surprise.

There, on the wooden floor slept a row of rosy apples, just like himself!

They were his brothers and sisters. They had never disappeared at all!

"Wake Up! Wake Up!" he squeaked in excitement.
"Wake Up!"

"It's Pipsy! It's Pipsy! He has found his way here at last!! Hooray!"

Everyone rolled around Pipsy, shouting and laughing and celebrating as only they knew how!

Then Pipsy remembered Silas. "Let me introduce Silas. He helped me to find you all!"

"Very glad to help!" Silas purred. "You enjoy yourselves!"

Silas left the Apple Family singing and dancing late into the night.

In the morning, as they all dozed, there was a heavy creak on the stairs.

Quickly, the Apple Family put themselves into a straight line.

They hardly dared to breathe.

These were not the gentle footsteps of the Farmer's Wife – no, these were hard and loud.

"What are all these silly apples doing here!" snarled a cross voice.

"I want to play with my train set. Get out of my way!"

Bobby, the Farmer's Son, picked up Pipsy, the apple closest to him, and threw him out of the window.

"Oh! Oh! Oh!" cried Pipsy. "Oh! Oh!

Ohhh......

Booomph! He landed hard in the middle of the farmyard. There were tractors turning with their loud engines. Pipsy tried to roll out of the way, but his rosy skin was bruised a horrible purple and he couldn't move.

What could he do? He would be crushed by those big wheels!

Then Pipsy felt a peculiar tickling on his back.

The tickling moved to his nose – *Atishoo!!*

"Whoaa! That was scary!" a tiny voice squeaked. "I nearly fell off!"

"Who are you?" said Pipsy.

"Oh, Hello Pipsy, I am Amanda Ant."

"How do you know my name?" said Pipsy.

"Oh, we all know you very well," said Amanda cheerily. "My brothers and sisters often wondered when you would get down from the old apple tree."

Pipsy sighed. "At least I was safe there! Not like here."

"Don't worry, we can sort this out," Amanda smiled. "Just a moment – back soon!"

Sure enough, Amanda was back in no time ... with hundreds and hundreds of tiny ants just like her.

"Ant Rescue here!" they all called. "Hold tight Pipsy."

Before he knew it, Pipsy was being carried by thousands of tiny ant feet.

To the sound of laughing and cheering squeaky voices, he was lifted far away from the farmyard tractors and into the safety of the orchard.

Ant Rescue placed him gently onto the soft grass.

"Now you relax. Go to sleep, and Get Well Soon!" smiled Amanda.

So Pipsy slept. He slept and he slept.

He slept all the next day.

He slept when the farmer dropped all the clippings from the lawn on top of him.

He did not wake up as Oscar slid quietly by, or hear Silas purring, "Miaoww, Hello Pipsy!" or Ned sniffing gently to see he was safe.

The Autumn leaves fell cosily around him.

The Winter snow covered him with a thick, warm, white blanket.

The Spring rain pattered softly.

The Summer sun shone brightly.

Pipsy slept and dreamed wonderful dreams.

He dreamed he was in the orchard and was as tall as the old apple tree.

He dreamed that he saw all his friends, Ned, Oscar, Silas, his brothers and sisters and Ant Rescue every day.

Then, one sunny morning he heard a lovely song.

"What a beautiful tune," he thought.

There, on a branch very close by, was a thrush.

"What a lovely voice," said Pipsy.

"Oh, you made me jump," said the thrush.
"What a fine perch you make, Mr. Apple Tree."

"Mr. Apple Tree? No, it's only me, Pipsy."

"Well ... you are a *little* Pipsy no more! You are the most splendid and most comfortable apple tree I have ever sung in! Pleased to meet you! My name is Speckle."

Speckle trilled loudly and there, to Pipsy's surprise, were all his friends, smiling and shouting across the orchard.

"Pipsy! Pipsy! Hello! Hello! You are awake! Hooray!"

Speckle whistled. Oscar smiled. Ned brayed,
"Well Done, young fellah!"

Amanda and Ant Rescue danced and squeaked on their thousands of tiny feet.

Silas purred and purred and purred.

"Hooray for Pipsy. Hooray for the most handsome apple tree in the whole orchard!" they all cheered.

"I'm the happiest and luckiest apple tree in the World to have such amazing friends like you!" said Pipsy.

"The best times are the BEST OF ALL times with friends like you!" he beamed contentedly.

Pipsy, Ned the donkey, Oscar the snail, Silas the cat, the Apple Family, Amanda Ant, Ant Rescue, and Speckle …

… would all like to thank Marian for telling their story so well.

They would also like to thank Andrew their illustrator
for making them look so good!

You will be glad to know that Bobby, the Farmer's
son, has been grounded and sent to his room for
being so mean and horrid!

The End

Printed in the United States
By Bookmasters